I've got a sore throat
and so has Bear.
Mum's taking us to
see the Doctor.

"Open wide
and say, Aaah!"
says Doctor.

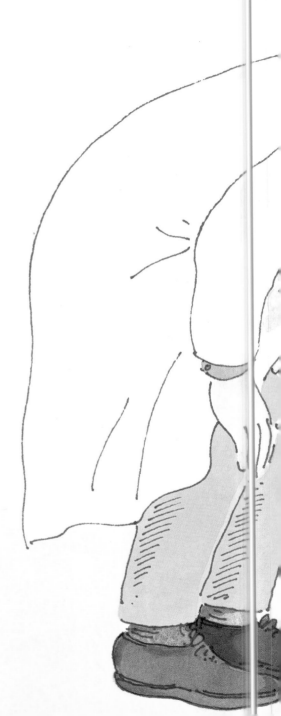

He looks into
our ears with
a little torch.

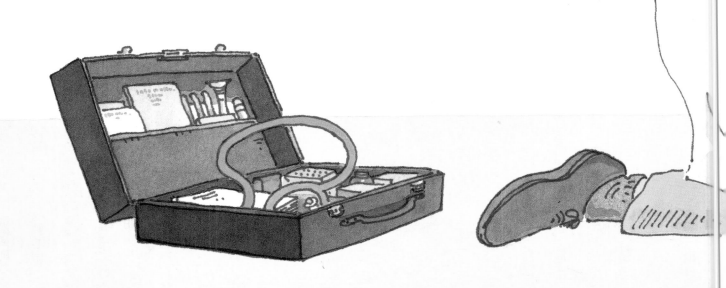

"Take a deep breath,"
says Doctor,
and he listens to
our chests with
his stethoscope.

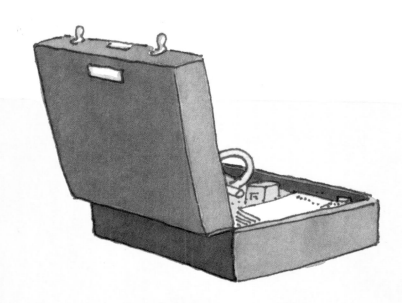

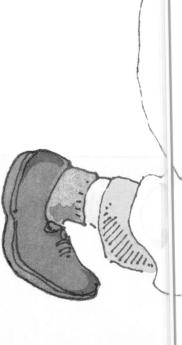

"Bear's fine, but this medicine will soon make you better, Freddie," says Doctor.

"Here you are, Freddie," says the chemist.

"Time for your medicine," says Mum. "You'll soon be well again."